Stay Away from
RAT BOY!

Laurie Lears

Illustrated by
Red Hansen

Albert Whitman & Company, Morton Grove, Illinois

For Wyatt—L.L.

For Rose, Alex, Cassie, and Pride 4—Thanks! —R.H.

Library of Congress Cataloging-in-Publication Data

Lears, Laurie.
Stay away from Rat Boy! / by Laurie Lears ; illustrated by Red Hansen.
p. cm.
Summary: Tyler is a bully who enjoys frightening other students, but when his only friend, his class's pet rat,
gets out of her cage he needs the help of a human friend, and fast.
ISBN 978-0-8075-6789-0
[1. Bullies—Fiction. 2. Rats as pets—Fiction. 3. Friendship—Fiction. 4. Schools—Fiction.]
I. Hansen, Red, ill. II. Title.
PZ7.L46365Std 2009 [E]—dc22 2008028086

Red Hansen created the illustrations by drawing, taking photos, and combining everything on his computer.
The design is by Carol Gildar.

For information about Albert Whitman & Company,
visit our web site at www.albertwhitman.com.

Tyler wasn't nice to the other kids at school.

He pushed in front of Kayla to get the first drink at the water fountain.

He snatched José's dessert away from him at lunch.

He laughed at Anthony when he dropped his marble collection during show and tell.

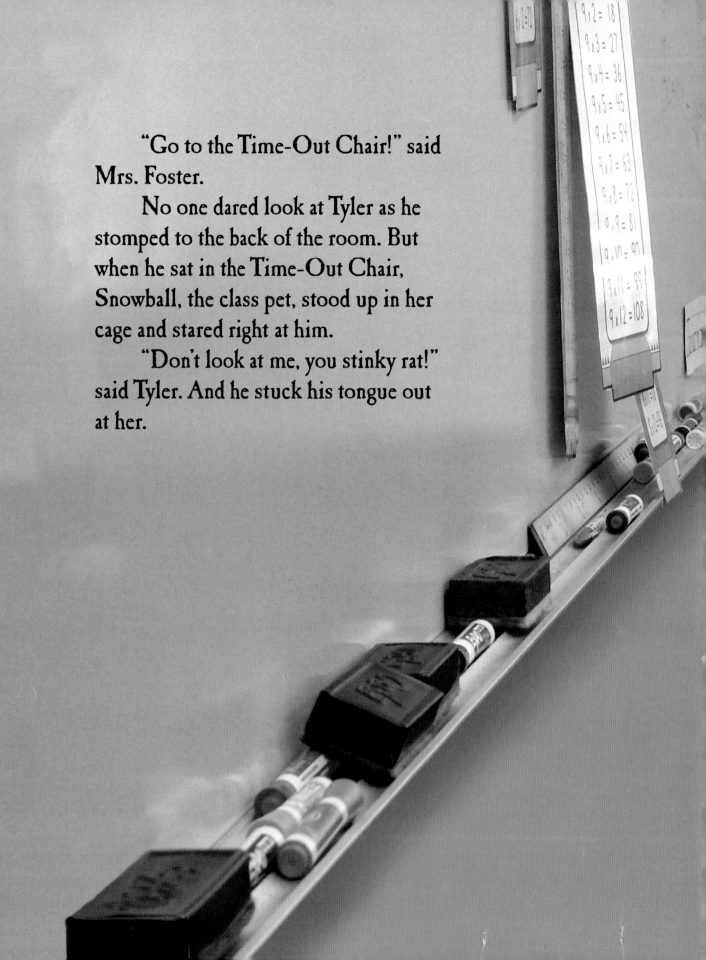

"Go to the Time-Out Chair!" said Mrs. Foster.

No one dared look at Tyler as he stomped to the back of the room. But when he sat in the Time-Out Chair, Snowball, the class pet, stood up in her cage and stared right at him.

"Don't look at me, you stinky rat!" said Tyler. And he stuck his tongue out at her.

Snowball didn't mind, though. She moved close
and sniffed him with her pink, quivering nose.

The next day Tyler had to sit in back of the room again. Snowball stretched out her paw and reached for him. This time, Tyler gently tapped his finger against the side of the cage and smiled.

When Mrs. Foster rearranged the children's desks,
Tyler got moved to a place where he could see Snowball
better. He noticed the way she washed her face with her
paws and how she curled her body into a tight ball before
going to sleep.

Tyler began to care about Snowball the way that she cared about him. He felt sad that she had to live alone in a little cage, so he brought her treats from home. Sometimes Mrs. Foster let him stay in from recess and play with Snowball. She scurried up his arms with her soft, tickly feet.

One afternoon Tyler was rubbing noses with Snowball, when José came in early from recess. Tyler's cheeks burned. He realized how silly he must look snuggling with a rat! He wanted to prove to José that he was tougher than ever.

"I'm Rat Boy!" cried Tyler. And he gnashed his teeth, clawed the air with his fingers, and chased José out of the room.

When Rat Boy's classmates heard his new name, they were more careful to keep out of his way. "Stay away from Rat Boy!" they told the younger students. "He's a bully!"

In the hallway, the children scooted aside when they saw Rat Boy coming. On the playground, they let him have first turn on the monkey bars and swings.

Mrs. Foster called Rat Boy to her desk. "The children are afraid to be around you," she said. "Let's talk about some ways you can be a better friend."

Rat Boy didn't want to talk. He liked to act tough. Besides, Snowball was the only friend he needed.

But one Monday morning Snowball was gone! Somehow she had opened her cage door and escaped! The children rushed off to look for her.

Rat Boy couldn't move.
His stomach hurt and tears
stung his eyes.

Days went by and there was no sign of Snowball.
Rat Boy's classmates seemed to forget about her.

But Rat Boy could think of nothing else. He
made posters and hung them around school:

He set out a trail of raisins
leading to Snowball's cage.
He worried that he might
never see her again.

Then one day Miss Gloria, the school cook, ran up to Rat Boy in the cafeteria. "Your rat is in our storage closet!" she cried. "Quick, bring a friend and come catch her!"

Rat Boy's heart pounded in his chest. He turned to ask Anthony for help, but Anthony picked up his tray and hurried away.

When he looked at Kayla, she ducked her head. "I . . . I have to finish eating my lunch," she said.

Rat Boy didn't know what to do. Someone had to help him catch Snowball!

Suddenly he felt a tap on his shoulder. "I'll help you," said José. "I like Snowball, too."

Rat Boy's eyes opened wide. He hadn't been kind to José . . . yet José was willing to help him.

"Let's go!" said Rat Boy. They dashed into the bright,
noisy kitchen and carefully opened the closet.
Snowball trembled in a corner.

Snowball raced around the closet, keeping out of the boys' reach. Finally she stopped to rest.

Rat Boy remembered he had two pieces of candy in his pocket. He unwrapped one piece and crept toward her. Snowball's whiskers twitched, and she sniffed the air. As she took a step toward the candy, Rat Boy cupped his hands around her and picked her up. Snowball was back at last!

Rat Boy and José put Snowball back in her cage. She didn't look happy. "I don't think she likes living in this little cage by herself," said Rat Boy. "I wish she could be free, but it's too dangerous."

"Maybe my dad will help us build a big cage for Snowball," said José. "Then we could get another rat to keep her company!"

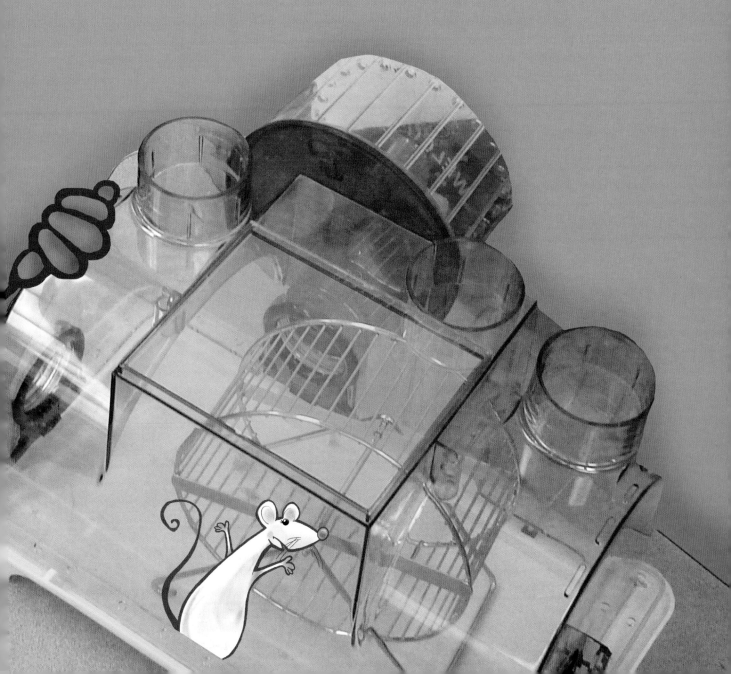

Rat Boy nodded. He liked José's idea. And he liked
José, too. He wished he hadn't been so mean to him.
"Thanks for helping me catch Snowball," he said.
"You can call me Tyler instead of Rat Boy, if you want to."

Then Tyler reached into his pocket and gave his last piece of candy to his new friend.